This edition published by Parragon Books Ltd in 2016

Parragon Books Ltd
Chartist House
15–17 Trim Street
Bath BA1 1HA, UK
www.parragon.com

ISBN 978-1-4748-3289-2

Printed in China

Disney

THE
LION KING

PaRragon

Bath • New York • Cologne • Melbourne • Delhi
Hong Kong • Shenzhen • Singapore

As the morning sun rose high over the
African plain, animals and birds gathered
at the foot of Pride Rock.

"There he is!" one of them cried
suddenly. "There's the new Prince!"
Everyone cheered and stamped their feet.
"Welcome Prince Simba!" they shouted.

They watched in silence as Rafiki, a wise old baboon, raised the lion cub high in the air. The clouds parted and the sun's rays shone down on the future King. Slowly Rafiki lowered his arms and took Simba back to his proud parents, King Mufasa and Queen Sarabi.

It was a very special day.

Time passed quickly for little Simba. There was so much to learn. One morning the King showed his son round the kingdom. "Remember," Mufasa warned, "a good king must respect all creatures, for we exist together in the great Circle of Life."

Later that day Simba met his uncle, Scar. The cub proudly told him that he had seen the whole of his future kingdom.

"Even beyond the northern border?" Scar asked slyly.

"Well, no," said Simba sadly. "My father has forbidden me to go there."

"Quite right," said Scar. "Only the bravest lions go there. An elephant graveyard is no place for a young prince."

Simba hurried away to find his best
friend, a young lioness called Nala.
Even though he knew it was wrong,
Simba had decided to visit the elephant
graveyard with Nala that very day.

He had no idea that Scar had ordered
three hyenas to go to the elephant
graveyard too. Scar wanted them to
kill the cub as the first step in his plan
to take over Mufasa's kingdom.

Simba raced ahead across the plains, leading Nala to the forbidden place. Eventually they reached a pile of bones and Simba knew they had arrived.

"It's creepy here." said Nala. "Where are we?"

"This is the elephant graveyard!" Simba cried. He was looking at a skull when he saw Zazu, his father's adviser.

"You must leave here immediately!" Zazu commanded. "You are in great danger."

But it was already too late! They were trapped. Three hyenas had surrounded them, laughing menacingly.

Simba took a deep breath and tried to roar – but only a
squeaky rumble came out. The hyenas laughed hysterically.

Simba took another deep breath.

ROAARR! The three hyenas looked round into the eyes
of – King Mufasa.

The hyenas fled howling into the mist.

Mufasa sent Nala and Zazu ahead and walked slowly home
with his son. "Simba, I'm disappointed in you. You disobeyed
me and put yourself and others in great danger."

Simba felt terrible. "I was only trying to be brave like you,"
he tried to explain.

"Being brave doesn't mean you go looking for trouble,"
said the King gently.

The moon shone brightly above them and the stars twinkled in the dark sky.

Mufasa stopped. "Look at the stars! From there the great kings of the past look down on us. Just remember that they'll always be there to guide you, and so will I."

Simba nodded. "I'll remember."

    By the next day Scar had devised another plan to get rid
of Mufasa and Simba. He led Simba to the bottom of a gorge
and told him to wait for his father. Then the hyenas started
a stampede among a herd of wildebeest.

    At that moment Mufasa was walking along a ridge with
Zazu. "Simba!" he cried. "I'm coming!"

    The King raced down the gorge and rescued his son, but
he could not save himself.

He fell onto an overhanging rock as the
wildebeest swept by him. Looking up he saw
his brother.

"Scar, help me!" he cried. But Scar just
leaned over and whispered, "Long live the
King!" Then he pushed Mufasa into the path
of the trampling wildebeest.

When the stampede was over, Simba ran to his father's side.

"Father," he whimpered, nuzzling Mufasa's mane. But the King did not reply, and Simba started sobbing.

"Simba," said Scar coldly, "what have you done? This is all your fault," he lied. "The King is dead and you must never show your face in the pride again. Run away and never return."

As Scar returned to take the royal throne at Pride Rock for himself, Simba stumbled exhausted and frightened through the grasslands towards the jungle. He took a few more shaky steps and collapsed. Hungry vultures circled above him.

Eventually Simba opened his eyes. A warthog,
called Pumbaa, and Timon, a meerkat, were gazing
down at him. They poured water into his dry mouth.
"You nearly died," said Pumbaa. "We saved you."

"Thanks for your help," said Simba, "but it doesn't matter. I've nowhere to go."

"Why not stay with us?" said Timon, kindly. "Put your past behind you. Remember! Hakuna matata – no worries! That's the way we live."

Simba thought for a moment and decided to stay in the jungle with his new friends.

Many years later, deep in a cave, Rafiki stared at a picture of a lion. "It is time," he said, smiling, and prepared to leave.

The very next day Simba rescued Pumbaa from a hungry lioness – it was Nala! The two friends were delighted to see each other again. Nala told Simba about Scar's reign of terror at Pride Rock and begged him to return. "With you alive, Scar has no right to the throne," she said.

"I can't go back. I'm not fit to be a king," Simba said sadly.

"You could be," Nala told him.

Simba showed Nala his favourite places
in the jungle. "It's beautiful," she said.
"I can see why you like it – but it's not your
home. You're hiding from the future." She
turned and left her friend alone.

That night Simba lay by a stream
thinking. He heard a noise and
looked up.

"Come with me," said Rafiki.
"I will take you to your father."

Simba followed him in wonder
to the edge of the stream. As Simba
looked into the water, his reflection
gradually changed shape and
became his father's!

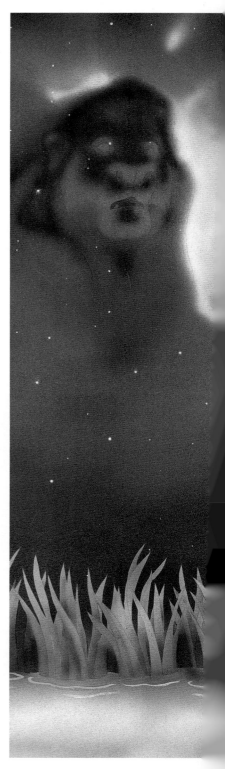

The reflection rose into the sky and
Simba heard Mufasa's voice:
"Simba. You must take your place in
the Circle of Life. You are my son and
the one true King." Then the reflection
and Rafiki disappeared.

Back at Pride Rock, the rains had been late coming and the land was dry. The hyenas paced impatiently round King Scar.

"We're starving," they howled. "The herds have gone. There's nothing left to eat."

Storm clouds gathered in the sky and a lightning bolt scorched the earth. As the dry grasses caught fire, flames swept towards Pride Rock. A lion appeared through the smoke. It was Simba!

Scar lunged at Simba, determined to kill him just as he had Mufasa. In the fierce battle that followed, Simba finally heaved Scar over the cliff face. Scar called to the hyenas to save him, but Nala and the lionesses drove them back. Simba was victorious!

Nala went to Simba's side. "Welcome home!" she whispered.

As they smiled at each other, it started to rain. The heavy drops soaked the dry ground and streambeds filled up once more. The plains came back to life and the herds returned.

One dawn the animals and birds made their way again to the foot of Pride Rock. Watched by the lions, Pumbaa and Timon, Rafiki picked up a tiny cub. He showed the new Prince – the son of King Simba and Queen Nala – to the cheering crowd below.

That night Simba watched the stars rise in the sky.
"Everything's all right, Father," he said softly. "You see,
I remembered." And the stars seemed to twinkle in reply.